Wine Country Writers' Festival

Anthology 2021

PRAIRIE SOUL PRESS

www.ThePrairieSoul.com/press

www.WineCountryWritersFestival.ca

Cover image: Kelly Visel

unsplash.com

Contents

Introduction … Faye Arcand   1

Fiction   3

The Day Jesus Came to Work … Svea Beson   5

Sweet Michael Sky … Andrea Heidebrecht   9

Fat Friday … Garry Litke   17

The Rhee Family Drugstore … Finnian Burnett   23

Poetry   29

Tireless Travail … Josephine LoRe   31

From the Farm Garden … Leanne Shirtliffe   33

evolution of word II … Laurie Anne Fuhr   35

August … Sally Quon   37

There will be Moths … Linda Hatfield   39

Non-Fiction   43

Eocene Walk … Donald V. Gayton   45

Stan, Alone in the Attic … Cherie Hanson   51

Prejudice & Necrotizing Enterocolitis …
Johanna Van Zanten   59

Copyrights   69

More   72

Introduction

... Faye Arcand

An-thol-o-gy -| ăn-thŏlə-jē -|(noun)

-|collection of selected writing

We at Wine Country Writers' Festival are pleased to share with you the winning entries in each category of the 1st Annual WCWF Writing Contest.

It isn't easy to throw your hat in the ring, so thank you for trusting us with your stories and poems. We offer our heartfelt congratulations to the winners and to all the entrants in this year's competition.

This festival and its writing contest are very much like the stories in this anthology.

It started with a simple spark which then morphed into an idea, the magnitude of which seemed impossible to tackle, but we made a conscious choice to move forward, and sketched out a draft.

Just like any writing or creative project, it can't happen without you.

A special thanks goes to our esteemed judges, Josephine LoRe (poetry), Simone Blais (nonfiction) and Lorna Schultz-Nicholson (fiction). Each judge took the time to comment on why they chose the included pieces. These comments offer insight for all writers, and we're grateful for their commitment.

A huge thank-you must also be given to our contest sponsor, The Raven's Oddities. The Raven's Oddities is a store in Okanagan Falls, B.C. that sells odd, unique antiques and eclectic items for those looking for something a little different. The owner/operator, Mike Arcand, donated all the prize monies for the WCWF Writing Contest, and we are very grateful.

Happy reading ... and then happy writing!

Faye Arcand,

Wine Country Writers' Festival organizer

Fiction

judged by Lorna Schultz Nicholson

The Day Jesus Came to Work

... Svea Beson

Honourable Mention

Jesus, help me! Please, just help me. What is wrong with me? Why is this my life?

I may have been hallucinating the day Jesus sat at my desk and told me to kill myself.

But why would I hallucinate Jesus? No idea. I'm not particularly religious, though I was brainwashed in the Catholic Church for the first eleven years of my life.

I've never been a big Jesus fan. Not like some. Aunties and Uncles being all praise Jesus and thank you Jesus for everything we have. I got what I have by working hard, nobody to thank but myself.

Yes, I wanted to die that day, it was all I could think about. The girls in the office talked about their kids, their husbands, and their dogs. I could not relate. I had nothing.

I sat there imagining eating sleeping pills like they were m and m's, puncturing my jugular with the utility knife I use to open mailboxes and many other life-ending scenarios.

When Jesus sat down, I thought I had truly lost my marbles, he wore the flowing robes, his beard was exactly as it should be. He looked calm, smiled like you'd imagine.

He said just do it. Stop being a pussy. No one will even notice. You keep talking about it, talk, talk, talk. Where's all the do, do, do.

Excuse fucking me?

Fuck you, Jesus.

This is none of your business, Jesus of the dollar store era. This is not your depression. This is not your agony, your daily pain, your every moment of self-loathing life. I will die when I want to die and on my own terms. I could live for another eighty years!

Well, fuck. He'd done it. Made me think to myself that I don't want to die. The nerve, making me

want to live. I was having a really good pity party over here.

You've done your job Jesus, go away. I didn't ask you here.

Oh, but you did. Don't you remember? You said, Jesus help me.

Lorna Schultz Nicholson's notes

This story was given an honourable mention because the last line caused a guffaw of laughter. As a reader, I never saw it coming and thought it worked.

Sweet Michael Sky
... Andrea Heidebrecht
Third Place

When the baby was finally out, I asked what he looked like.

"A real mess," Brennon said. But I knew newborns never looked like the chubby, pink ones you see in the movies. Our baby screamed something awful while the nurse cleaned him up. She wrapped him in a white blanket with stripes of pink and blue, then placed him gently on my chest. He was perfect.

"What are you going to call him?" she asked, sounding so bored I figured she'd asked that same question hundreds of times before.

The baby had Brennon's fair skin and blond hair and my nose and forehead. He had his eyes squeezed shut, but when I ran my hand over his tiny head he blinked, and I glimpsed the most beautiful blue eyes I'd ever seen. The name came to me just like that. "Sky," I said.

"I'm sorry?" the nurse asked, a little too politely.

"I'm going to call him Sky. Because his eyes are the most amazing blue."

"Come on, Chloe," Brennon said. "We're not naming him something stupid."

"Of course, the name is your choice." The nurse looked from me to Brennon. "But there's a good chance his eyes will darken up."

Brennon leaned over my shoulder to get a better look at the baby. "His name will be Michael," he decided. Brennon hated how unusual his own name was. When we were in high school and already together, he'd made everyone call him Brandon for three months before his dad found out and knocked him around for it. He said if Brennon wanted to be called something else, he could think of plenty of words to use. At school after that Brennon ignored anyone who called him Brandon, and soon no one did. It was funny how quickly it seemed like nothing had ever changed.

I didn't want to upset Brennon, but I wasn't about to give in all the way either. Later, when the nurse handed me the papers, I wrote "MICHAEL SKY" in capital letters and handed them back to her before Brennon could see. I knew in my heart it was the right name for my baby.

Sweet Michael Sky was the best little baby I could have imagined. He slept through the night almost right away, and he didn't make much of a fuss when he was wet or hungry. I would spend whole afternoons sitting on the couch, just holding him and staring into his eyes, which—despite what the nurse said—had stayed the most gorgeous blue.

When Michael Sky was about eight months old, my sister stopped by to visit. Kenzie lived nearby, and I'd texted a few times since I'd had my baby, but this was the first time she'd shown any interest in meeting him. So that's how I knew something was up even before she flashed her shiny new engagement ring at me. It was at least three times as big as the one on my own finger and not cloudy at all.

We'd been sitting awkwardly at my second-hand kitchen table while I listened to Kenzie gloat endlessly about her handsome fiancé and her plans for a fancy wedding when she suddenly paused, and I sensed her mood shift. She slid her gaze over my outdated cupboards, then asked, "Aren't you going back to work?"

Her heavy perfume had a sharpness to it that stung my nose with each breath I took. I held my coffee cup in front of my face, trying to block the stench, but it was useless. I shrugged. "I like being home with the baby. Plus, Brennon likes me home."

She moved closer to me, and I tried not to lean away from the even stronger sting of her perfume. "Does Brennon make enough for you to do that?" I knew she was trying to cover the sarcasm in her voice, but I still heard it. It was none of her business how much we struggled each month. Brennon had been owed a raise for a while, and as soon as that came through things would be easier. But I wasn't about to admit that to my sister.

She waited for me to say something, and when I didn't, she sat back in her seat, narrowing her heavily made-up eyes. I knew she wasn't finished coming at me yet. This was our normal. She'd throw knives at me, and I'd dodge them until she left me alone.

"Are you going to tell me what's wrong with your baby?" she said.

"What do you mean?" I asked, glancing over at my boy to make sure he hadn't tipped over in his chair. When we'd rented this house, the owner had called the layout "open concept," but really what it meant was the place was too tiny to fit walls in everywhere. The baby was in the living room, but he was only a few feet away from where Kenzie and I sat at the kitchen table. Michael Sky was still sitting quietly where I'd set him. He'd been an angel the whole visit.

"I've been here for an hour, and he's been staring at the TV the whole time. That's weird, Chloe. And can't he sit on his own yet? He's way too big for that bouncy chair."

"He's just a good baby, is all." I told her. "He loves his chair." Kenzie worked in a daycare and thought she knew everything about babies, even though she hadn't had her own yet.

"If I were you, I'd definitely get him tested," she said, getting up and walking over to the counter behind me. I hoped she wasn't this rude to the parents of her daycare kids, but then I knew she would never talk like this to anyone else. As long as I could remember she'd always been resentful of me, and I could never figure out why. I hadn't been my mom's favourite, so there was no cause for jealousy there. Both of us irritated our mother in the same way: always making noise in the house or needing something from her. Kenzie left home a few months before I did, and mom didn't try to hide how relieved she was when I told her I was moving out to marry Brennon.

"Tested for what?" I asked, getting up to pour myself more coffee as she sat back in her seat with a full cup. When I saw that she'd emptied the pot, I made a new one though I was already jittery from too much caffeine. I needed to keep my hands busy to stop from saying something I'd regret later. Kenzie had found her mark, but I was determined not to show it.

"Never mind," she said. "I shouldn't have said anything." She giggled, and I realized she already knew she'd gotten to me. She was being her nasty old self, but I couldn't help wondering if she'd seen something in my baby.

When I sat back down at the table, she was staring at her ring again and tilting her hand all around to catch the light in her diamonds. I could see it sparkling from where I sat.

"It sure is nice," I said, trying to get back on her good side.

"I know. And it's ten times nicer than the one Mason bought for Sierra last year."

I hesitated, not sure why she'd brought up her fiancé's ex. "Mason doesn't still see her, does he?" I asked.

She shrugged. "I'm not stupid. But if he gives me what I want, why should I care? We're going to Spain for our honeymoon." She set her cup down with a clunk, and some coffee spilled onto the table. "I won't have to work after we're married either."

I didn't know how to reply to what she'd said, so I kept my mouth shut. She mistook my silence as judgment. "Oh, what do you know?" she said. "You sit here all day in your crappy little house, and you think you have it better than me?" She stood and grabbed her purse from the couch. "When you get my invitation," she added, "let me know if you need to borrow a dress from my closet. We both know you can't afford anything half-decent to wear to my wedding." She went out the door and slammed it behind her.

Michael Sky stared at the TV, not reacting to anything that had gone on around him. I unbuckled the belt of his chair and held him to me, breathing in the sweet smell of his hair that was like balm to the inside of my nose. I sang softly to him as I carried him upstairs and laid him in his crib, and I didn't leave his room until he was fast asleep.

Brennon came in all dirty and cranky from work like usual. I didn't want to tell him I was worried about the baby right then, but when I told him Kenzie had been by, he figured she'd been causing trouble.

"So now she has you worried about the baby?" Brennon said like he couldn't believe how low Kenzie had gone this time. "She's just jealous her little sister had a baby before her."

He was probably right, but I told him I'd made a doctor's appointment for Michael Sky anyway. Brennon's face began to redden, and I knew I'd made him angry. I spoke quickly. "I'm just trying to do what's best for him," I said, less sure of myself. "Isn't that what you want, too?"

He threw his hands up in the air. "How am I supposed to know what's best for him?"

I didn't reply because that's what I wondered, too. How could he know? How could I? Neither of us had good role models growing up, and we didn't have anyone to look to for advice now. We were Michael Sky's whole world, but we were only ever guessing at how to make it good. I felt like I was back in high school, but I was writing an exam for a class I'd never taken. And I wouldn't find out if I passed or failed until at least eighteen years later.

We stood in silence, staring at each other, until he spoke again. "There's nothing wrong with my son," he said quietly. Then he turned and went back out, still in his work uniform. I heard the car start and drive away.

I stood alone for a few minutes wondering if I should cancel the appointment. Then I climbed the stairs to the baby's room and leaned over the rail of the crib. Michael Sky was wide awake and babbling softly. He grinned when I tickled his belly with my fingertips. And I knew then that I would never stop trying to do what was right for him, even if I wasn't sure what that was.

Lorna Schultz Nicholson's notes

This was a story that seemed on all fronts to have a "sweet" focus, but very strategically had an underlying message about the love a mother feels for a child. The theme in this story was done in such a way that the reader wasn't banged over the head but given a main character who was real about her feelings. The scene between Chloe (main character) and her sister was interesting and through dialogue the reader was given a glimpse into Chloe's past, giving the story depth. In the beginning the author paints Chloe to be naïve but then the reader is shown her strength. The character development of Chloe was the most intriguing part of this story, as the author allowed her to grow.

Fat Friday

... Garry Litke

Second Place

I peered over the top of my work cubicle to determine the source of the tantalizing fast-food aroma. It was Brenda, that bitch. She was wolfing down full-meal deal at her desk, slurping a shake and popping fries into her mouth while hamburger sauce oozed obscenely from the corner of her mouth. She stared at her computer screen as her jaws worked mechanically.

I calculated. Burger 900 calories, french fries 470, and milkshake 850. Brenda consumed more in ten minutes than I permitted myself in three days. It wasn't fair.

Supervisor Bob emerged from his corner office carrying a green assignment folder. As he passed Brenda's desk, he snitched a fry and gave her a salacious wink.

Disgusting.

I plopped my ample rump into my ergonomic chair and picked up a carrot stick just as the green folder landed on my desk.

"I need this contract prepared by 4:00 pm," Bob said, the smile gone from his face. No lunchtime levity for me anymore. And he'd rejected my latest bid for promotion. As I opened the folder and began to decipher his handwriting, my blood boiled at how Brenda's arrival had changed things in this office. We were a conservative publisher of a popular religious magazine, and we'd always kept to ourselves. She'd stirred things up by encouraging everyone to connect on Facebook, forcing us to become more socially interactive. I didn't like it until I discovered that I could troll my new "friends", snooping into their extended network of contacts. I'm not a Peeping Tom, but in this case, I felt like Sherlock Holmes, using a new tool to learn interesting facts about people.

I'd found a posting from three years ago where someone named Alicia had tagged Brenda in a photo. The image, preserved forever, showed Brenda bent over the counter of a neon-lit tattoo parlor, red lace panties barely covering her butt. Black eyeliner drooped over her unfocused eyes, and purple lipstick smudged a suggestively opened mouth as she gazed over her shoulder at the camera.

Baked.

A red-bearded tattoo artist—surrounded by drunks cheering appreciatively—leered into the camera lens, apparently satisfied with the newly completed "tramp stamp" on Brenda's backside. It featured a chilling visage of a monstrous black cat with tufted brows and Satanic red eyes. Narrow-slit pupils invited a pornographic peep into the forbidden valley below.

Gross.

"A fun way to finish Brenda's bachelorette party," the caption read. "Wedding in two weeks!"

Apparently, evidence of extreme intoxication and an ugly tattoo had finished more than just a party. Brenda remained unmarried. Her straight-laced employers would not be impressed either.

Yesterday, I'd screen-shot the photo to my phone and printed a color enlargement at Staples. Now, I retrieved the picture from my backpack, slipped it into the green folder, and skirted surreptitiously into the coffee room. No one there. Perfect.

In seconds, I'd taped it securely to the fridge and returned to my desk, poker-face firmly in place.

When my co-workers returned from lunch, they paraded into the staff room to fill their coffee mugs as fortification for an afternoon in their cubicles. A rumble of laughter rolled from the room, followed by excited, but muted, conversation. They returned to their desks, hilarity suppressed, wearing guilty looks like those of a pubescent teenager who'd discovered dad's stash of porno magazines.

I waited, pretending to be focused at my computer.

At 1:24 pm, according to the clock on my screen, Brenda carried the garbage from her fast-food lunch into the staff room for disposal. We all heard her scream. Several people, including Bob, rushed into the staff room find out what happened. Did she fall or injure herself? Seconds later she burst out with the humiliating photo crumpled in her white-knuckled fist, followed by a less-than-sympathetic group exchanging embarrassed glances.

Brenda grabbed her backpack and stormed out of the office with a slam. Supervisor Bob slid back to his corner enclave and quietly closed the door.

At five o'clock, I donned the beige sweater hanging from the back of my chair and strode blank-faced toward the exit, avoiding a small group of gossipers who were exchanging whispered conversation.

On the way home, I stopped at a supermarket for my Friday night treat, a tub of fat-free, caramel-pecan ice-cream, only 240 calories per cup. I carried it to my apartment, measured out a cupful, and then relaxed at the kitchen table while I spooned the creamy, cold confection onto my tongue.

Mmmmm.

When it was gone, I turned to my laptop and clicked on Facebook, scrolling through my list of new friends until I found Bob Simpson. Supervisor Bob the philanderer. Married. Happy family. Churchgoer.

Someone had tagged him in an old photo, at a rally shaking hands with KKK leader David Duke. A cross burned in the background. Interesting.

My face broadened into a smile of satisfaction. The corner office would soon be mine.

Lorna Schultz Nicholson's notes

This story was well written, and the author used colorful language and some wonderful showing to create the main character. Here is an example of the great showing in this story, "I plopped my ample rump into my ergonomic chair and picked up a carrot stick just as the green folder landed in my lap." Right from the first paragraph, the scenes were descriptive and visual, allowing the reader to form an immediate picture. The main character was flawed, and that worked for the story, and the author was successful at having the inner thoughts of the character stay true to the character. The author carried the flaws right to the end of the story and ended with a last line that held punch. The title for this story was excellent.

The Rhee Family Drugstore

… Finnian Burnett

First Place

Cheap fluorescent lights turn even the warmest autumn tones ghastly shades of death white. The mirror is slightly warped so even without the sickly pallor, my face looks lumpy and strange. The person in the mirror is ugly and exhausted. I brush my teeth and wash my face and hair as best I can in the small sink.

Back in the stock room, I rummage carefully around the shelves for a warm Gatorade. I down half then refill with water from the sink. My pack is under the last shelf, hidden behind a box of cassette tapes Mr. Rhee truly believed were coming back in vogue.

"Sela." He had been excited, shouting. "Kids today like everything old. Record players. Tea. We'll make a fortune." When he yelled, his accent got so thick, I could barely understand him. I hadn't the heart to tell him no one was coming to the Rhee Family Drug to buy 1980s cassette tapes.

I pull out my pack and reach for the vitamins. I can justify stealing a Gatorade every day since Mr. Rhee hasn't given me a raise in four years, but I bought the vitamins with money from my own paycheck. They're the cheapest multi-vitamin we carry and the most I can afford.

I pop one in my mouth and swallow it. If I end up not eating anything today, I'm still getting my daily nutrients. I run a quick comb through my hair and pull clean clothes out of my pack before pushing everything back behind the box of tapes. Even if we have a run on cassettes, Mr. Rhee will send me to drag out these boxes. His knees don't work well anymore, and he saves any task that involves squatting for me.

On the other side of the stock room, across from the inventory shelves, there's a long row of bright red smocks. I run my hand along them, and press my face against the sleeves, breathing in the fresh smell. Mr. Rhee and I wear them while the store is open, and he sends them to his sister's laundry once a week. When I was twelve, skinny and boyish with choppy haircuts courtesy of my mom, I hated this polyester addition to my overall ridiculous and awkward appearance. At sixteen with few other options to my wardrobe, I appreciate the clean uniform. Slipping into one of the smocks feels like wearing a scratchy, but pleasant hug. I breathe in the detergent again and go out to the main floor to open the store.

Mr. Rhee rolls in at ten. I was fourteen when Mrs. Rhee died, and I got a promotion. Mr. Rhee was crying when he gave me a key, but all he said was, "You open. I close." Mrs. Rhee once told me they had a son who killed himself before I started working there. He closes at nine, but he hangs around until midnight, cleaning, straightening the shelves, coming up with new bad ideas to improve business. He doesn't sleep much. I leave at five PM and come back at 2 AM. I don't want to risk sneaking back in while Mr. Rhee is still there.

"Sela," he says, as he walks up to the counter. "Customers?"

"One. A lady bought some aspirin and a wind chime."

Mr. Rhee smiles, delighted. "I knew they would sell."

"We've sold exactly two of them."

"It takes time," he says.

"It's been eighteen months."

He tsks at me. Eternally hopeful. I almost think I could tell him, but I know what he'd say. "Go home. Tell your mom." Mr. Rhee doesn't talk about it, but I know he's big on family.

At half past eleven, I sell two packs of toilet paper, a long-handled bath brush, and a bottle of eye drops. Mr. Rhee locks the front door and asks me to meet him in the stock room.

I creep in, a lump settling in the back of my throat. He's sitting at the small table near the smocks, my pack on the table in front of him. The question is on his lips, but I can tell he doesn't know how to ask. A look of bewilderment crosses his face and for a wild moment, I think he's going to cry.

"Just tell me, Sela," he says so softly I almost think I imagined it.

"I was kicked out." I glance to judge his reaction. "And I'm pregnant."

He looks down at the Gatorade bottle and the pack of generic vitamins.

I stand up straighter, pulling down on the hem of my smock. "I take a vitamin and a Gatorade every day. I clean up after myself. I paid for the vitamins." My hands feel monstrous; I don't know where to put them while I stand here. "I've stolen all the Gatorades."

"Sela," he says, his voice barely above a whisper. "How are you pregnant? You don't even have a…"

He pauses and I wonder if he's thinking of my stepfather, whose voice boomed across the store whenever he'd come pick me up. The deep bruises his fingers sometimes left on my arm. The way he held me as he guided me out the door. I remember turning back once to look at Mr. Rhee and seeing his lips pursed with fear and disapproval.

I can see the memories flashing across his face and I know he's ashamed. He's going to fire me; he's going to take my key. He's going to send me back to my mom and my stepdad and I'll be stuck there, raising my baby, making myself as invisible as I can.

He stands up and turns away from me, gazing at the long row of shelves in front of him. He reaches for something and turns back around. "My son's room is still…" he stops, swallows. "It needs to be cleaned," he says briskly. "It will be nicer than the stock room floor." He puts something into my hand and heads back to the store. "We'll talk about a raise during dinner tonight."

Is he asking me to move in? I stare after him, willing myself not to cry, not to make a scene. When he's gone, I look down at the item in my hand. Prenatal vitamins. I slip them into the pocket of my smock and head back to the floor.

Lorna Schultz Nicholson's notes

This was a touching story, and the writer did a wonderful job of creating emotion, and a beautiful relationship between an older man and a teen. The two main characters were real and honest, the relationship heartwarming, and that was what made the story stand out. The dialogue between Sela and Mr. Rhee was crisp, clean and gave the reader so much information about both characters. The plot built in this short story, and the author didn't give everything away in the beginning, allowing the reader to be intrigued. The story arc was well done, as the author grew the tension step-by-step until it hit the climax at the right moment. The ending worked and the last line was magic. It was the perfect show don't tell moment.

Poetry

judged by Josephine LoRe

Tireless Travail

... Josephine LoRe

Judge's Poem

To hear the wind and know there are no answers
To see dragonfly in flight, singly or paired
    double-winged, blue, green
Butterfly of orange and rust, rainforest-born
    another black-winged, laced in white

To know that everything in this forest
      this thousand shades of green and brown
        is living
       and when these plants lay down their lives
           they nurture the next

      they are always alive

      Yellow jacket, mosquito, fly
mushroom frilling mossy stump

Lilypads
     golden smudges on the blackness
           of the surface of the pond

This pond created by beaver
                    the tireless travail

To know the pond created by beaver
        but not see beaver
                To know the tireless travail
            of creation

From the Farm Garden

... Leanne Shirtliffe

Honorable Mention

All summer, dirt housed under fingernails,
wide and flat as sections of wheat, oats, canola.

All summer, hands grew in size and silence.
"Talk is for people who don't work hard," they said,
for dinner tables after the grain is sold,
for when the malt is in the bottle.

All summer, her hair ripened like bearded barley.
She biked with the wind, down well-worn tracks
of gravel roads until a bladed grader erased
the only path she thought she knew.

All summer, she dirtied her hands: by picking Portulaca
that encroached upon row upon row of radishes,
carrots, kohlrabi; by relishing the cucumbers'
velvet-leaved caresses, how their yellow blooms
transformed to quarts of dills and bread-and-butters,

how their vines extended past the sprawling garden,

an insouciance preserved by the rubber jar seals
she'd steal to elastic back her wide-leg jeans as she rode
half-haloed, half-laughing into the silent wind
with dirt under her fingernails.

Josephine LoRe's notes

This poem deserves honourable mention as there are
many promising components: the rich descriptions, the
repetitions and well-crafted alliterations (row upon row of
radishes / carrots, kohlrabi) the fresh and beautiful
phrasing: her hair ripened like bearded barley, the
cucumbers' / velvet-leaved caresses, as she rode / half-
haloed, half-laughing into the silent wind.

evolution of word II

... Laurie Anne Fuhr

Third Place

in the beginning was the word.
or was it a grunt? there was one word
and it meant everything. God, existing before
the people She made who invented language,
gave a high holy ummph and the power came on.
grunted again, and Adam and Eve
had to find some clothes, rent an apartment.

before it even found the mouth of God,
the word learned to walk before it could run—
but first it swam. the word swam around awhile,
figured out different kinds of swimming—
the front stroke, the back stroke, strokes of genius.
the word grew nubs. evolution is the distance
between two states of being, between
tadpole school and nubementary.

the word wasn't the best student.
yet, inevitability worked in their favour.
nubs got longer, sprang feet, wet and webbed.
they grew a spine, then feet. legs developed

to relieve awkwardness. all that studying
paid off, even before currency was invented.
the word was rich with growth.

that was when God opened Her mouth
and sucked in like a great vacuum,
or like She was trying to suck a milkshake
out of a skinny straw because
they'd run out of wide ones,
or like every volcano erupting backwards.
into Her mouth went the grunt
that would become the word,
the word that made the world.
in a word, we made Her.
now the word was Hers to make us with.

Josephine LoRe's notes

I was intrigued by this poem, the evolution of the word. It
is the second part of a two-part poem, but I believe stands
well on its own. Here are some of the expressions I found
particularly compelling: words you speak / carry traces of
liver, viscera, coronary sap; words you edit, words you
exit; I open my mouth and forgive my body; I open my
mouth and read a poem, / very softly, into your collar.

There is very effective use of repetition, and this would
be wonderful as a Spoken Word piece. This poet shows a
lot of promise in the uniqueness of perspective and
expression.

August

... Sally Quon

Second Place

winding mountain road
dust in the darkness
new moon rising
nexus of night
beyond moss-covered canyon walls
to battle-scarred ground
remnants of last year's burn
wind   whistling over rocky ground
shivering in the grass
we lay in
silence
as stars
fell from the sky
unhindered
by the dreams
of mortals
or pain of love

Josephine LoRe's notes

This poem is descriptive and evocative, deeply rooted in nature and also thrumming with human emotion: desire, fear, and pain. I love the simplicity of the phrasing, like an impressionistic painting—dust in darkness, wind whistling over rocky ground, as stars / fell from the sky. There is also a sense of movement as the mind's eye is led from one image to the next and at the end, the poignancy of the humans laying "shivering in the grass", in silence. How haunting the final verses … stars / unhindered / by the dreams / of mortals / or pain or love.

I also think this poem was aptly titled, August for the month of the Perseid meteor showers, when the skies are indeed filled with falling stars, and also the adjective august, meaning marked by majestic dignity or grandeur, inspiring reverence and admiration, whether this second meaning was intentional or simply a fortuitous coincidence.

There will be Moths

... Linda Hatfield

First Place

When these dreary days
        withdraw,
when worries lift
and hearts unclench
and breath resumes
its soothing rhythm,
there will be family
and rejoicing 'round
the table once again.

When this long twilight
ends,
when shadows melt
and hope returns
and eyes refocus
on the dawn,
there will be songs
and circle dancing 'round
the bonfires of the night.

Bats will swoop and

wolves will watch—
             restless
as the stars that sing us
back into the light.
And the tambourine moon
will rise and shimmer
while around the glow
of a brighter future,
there will be moths—
paper wings beating
in a futile circle,
reminders of what we stand to
suffer
should we forget
to look away
or become
blind
to all we've learned
and lost.

Josephine LoRe's notes

This poem resonates with me and warrants rereading to
unriddle the meaning of the rich and subtle imagery. I love
the lyrical elements (the sound devices in the repetitions
and alliterations), the structure, the quiet rhythms, the
metaphor, the theme, and the uniqueness of certain
phrasing. Most of all, I love the overriding message: the
unconquerable hope that this darkness will be vanquished
by the light and that notwithstanding the suffering, there

is a lesson to be learned. It could be read as a COVID-based poem but truly has a broader universality.

Certain phrases that stood out for me were: restless / as the stars that sing us / back into the light, the tambourine moon, moths— / paper wings beating. I appreciate as well the mystery of the title, There Will be Moths.

Non-Fiction

judged by Simone Blais

Eocene Walk

... Donald V. Gayton

Third Place

A short walk through a tony Kelowna neighborhood has layers of meaning for me. This walk is taken by an unspoken fellowship of Cancer Center patients who shun the expensive hospital parkade, and who don't mind the five-block walk in exchange for free neighborhood parking. Another meaningful walk for me is in the White Lake Basin, about a hundred kilometers south. The two walks are separated by 50 million years and joined by a tree.

During the Eocene Epoch the White Lake Basin and other parts of BC supported lush semi-tropical vegetation. The signature tree species of that Epoch was metasequoia, also known as the dawn redwood. On my walks in this quiet, introspective Basin I have collected a few fossil samples of that tree's unique feather-shaped leaves. They are encased in light gray sandstone, and perfectly preserved. The leaves themselves are jet-black, paper-thin precursors of coal.

I was dimly aware of the history of metasequoia, assumed to be extinct until a Chinese botanist named

Wang Zhan found a single grove of it in a remote corner of Sichuan Province in 1943. But in my ignorance, I had no idea the tree had gone on to become a well-known domestic landscaping specimen. The revelation came on one of my Kelowna cancer walks. As I passed the front yard of an upscale home, there was a metasequoia, instantly recognizable and big as life. The tree's foliage, a kind of hybrid cross between needles and leaves, triggered the shock of recognition. I was dumbfounded. In a brief trespass, I nipped off a single leaflet and carefully placed it in my pocket notebook. Returning home from the Cancer Center, I went immediately to lay the fresh leaf alongside my fossil samples. Despite the 50 million years they were absolutely, and stunningly, identical.

The first person to describe metasequoia fossils in the BC Interior was George Mercer Dawson (1849-1901). Growing up in Central Canada, Dawson spent much of his short adult life exploring the Canadian West. An indefatigable traveller, geologist, anthropologist, writer and photographer, Dawson collected in the fossil-rich terrain around Princeton, BC, on the Similkameen River. He sent his fossil samples back to his father Sir John William Dawson, professor of Geology at McGill University in Montreal. Both father and son were eminent Canadian scientists, and their careers overlapped, in both time and interests. Having received the samples, the elder Dawson described and sketched his son's Princeton metasequoia, stating:

"The above species are sufficient to indicate an abundance of coniferous trees in the vegetation that surrounded the ancient Similkameen Lake."

This illustrious father, Sir John Dawson, was a bundle of contradictions. Broadly educated, progressive and an expert on fossil flora, he was also a devoted Presbyterian and staunch creationist, totally rejecting Charles Darwin's recent theories of the ascent of man from hominid ancestors. To the elder Dawson, a Darwinian human would be a repugnant, amoral beast, bent on destroying nature. The younger George Dawson was never explicit about his opinions on human evolution, but there is no doubt he quietly accepted Darwin's theory. In one of his private notebooks penned later in life, he made an oblique comment on how he dealt with father-son philosophical differences: "I live behind entrenchments and in fortifications fancied by myself." Young George contracted tuberculosis of the spine as a child and spent years in painful rehabilitation. The illness twisted his body and stopped its growth. He was, probably as a result, not comfortable in society. Upon completing university, he spent most of the rest of his life in the Canadian wilderness. Ideological differences with his father may have played a role in Dawson's choice of careers. He differed from his father not only on human evolution, but on religion as well. In one of his poems (again, not for publication) he mused:

When alone I turn
To where the lights of heaven burn
My lips refuse to utter prayer

In the annals of complex and tortuous father-son relationships, the Dawson story stands by itself.

I am no stranger to father-son disputes, experiencing a decade-long falling-out with my own father over my resistance to America's involvement in the Vietnam War, and the military draft that supported it. He and I remained far distant from each other, within our respective ideological fortifications. I feel a kinship: both George Mercer Dawson and I landed in the British Columbia Interior for reasons of belief. Or the lack thereof.

Turmoil, both personal and national, threads through the metasequoia story. Wang Zhan the botanist spent years on the run in his own country, dodging Japanese invaders. In 1943 he joined Chiang Kai-Shek's new Kuomintang government as a forester. During one of his inspection tours in the central part of the country, a bout of malaria forced him to stop and recuperate in a small village. While there, he heard about an unusual tree species growing in the rugged mountains nearby. Recuperating, he hiked out to see the grove, and the rest is history.

There are a daunting number of subdivisions within Kingdom Plantae but highlighting a few illustrates metasequoia's unique position. It is a conifer, or cone bearer. Conifers are evergreen, with a few notable exceptions: larch, tamarack and metasequoia are deciduous, shedding their foliage every fall. Nearly all conifers have needle-like leaves except, not surprisingly, metasequoia.

I am not altogether sure what meaning to draw from this 50-million-year personal foliage coincidence. How could I have not known that metasequoia is now a relatively common landscape tree? Or should I marvel at the amazing durability of nature's creatures? Or the humbling of the human race by this ancient tree? Or the insignificance of my medical situation, an old man with low-grade prostate cancer, compared to the grand scheme of human conditions?

The metasequoia has two coniferous evergreen cousins, the enormously tall coast redwood, found intermittently along the California and Oregon coasts, and the famous, long-lived giant sequoia of California's Sierra mountains. The scientific name of metasequoia is Metasequoia *glyptostroboides*, which of course is laden with meanings not accessible to us mortals. But the prefix meta- does speak to me. Its Latin definition is beyond, or transcendent.

When I do the cancer walk, starting from free parking, past the metasequoia and along the five blocks to the Sindi Ahluwalia Hawkins Cancer Centre, I am part of the unspoken fellowship. We are all heading there for either diagnosis, consultation, chemotherapy or radiation. Fellowship continues in the radiation waiting rooms, where we trade magazines, offer up our chair next to the window, or chat about many subjects except the obvious one. Our famed Canadian politeness is much in evidence here. On the coffee table in the waiting room is a massive 3000-piece jigsaw puzzle which takes several days to complete, each patient fitting a few pieces. When the puzzle is finally finished a staffer disassembles it, takes the box to an adjacent waiting room, and the process starts over.

I am keenly aware of my trivial membership in this community since prostate cancer is rarely fatal. As the saying goes, many men die with prostate cancer, but few die of it. That token membership is forcefully driven home to me whenever I pass a middle-aged woman wearing the telltale headscarf. But like the metasequoia, Wang Zhan and the younger Dawson, we are unique, and we all soldier on.

Simone Blais's notes

There is something incredibly satisfying when a writer's interest in a topic borders on obsession, and that fascination is folded into a greater narrative. The metasequoia carries profound meaning as the narrator navigates their mortality, a resonant metaphor rooted in the change-filled era in which the tree species thrived.

Stan, Alone in the Attic

... Cherie Hanson

Second Place

Stan was one of those lurking in the shadow type boys that was excluded or withdrew or was happier standing outside the gathered normals. He was a social anthropologist, an intellectual, a quietly curious unremarkable being. His thin, curved spine signaled years of formation around one book and then the next.

He was so perfectly camouflaged that I didn't notice him for the entire year. He, was, of course a senior and shelved in a higher, out of reach level than I occupied as a mere Junior. Different grades had little opportunity to connect. There were too many of us to emerge as real people while we rushed through the halls, passed along the breeze way heedlessly designed to be open to the lashing of the elements of constant rain and wind.

In my high school, your grade was as socially structure as is any ridged caste system in a third world country. In many ways, those three years were systematically machining us to fit a slot in the system. Subcultures held territory. The drug smoking intellectuals sat in full lotus on the flat roof above the science lab. We all discovered their phantom existence when one of them fell off of the edge and broke his leg. I was sitting in the biology lab. I saw him fly past the window.

These outcasts would go on to run companies, create systems and refuse the constructs of boundaries the rest of us followed without even knowing there was an alternative.

Under the bleachers lurked the nefarious under achievers. Things happened under there that my protestant middle class entity could never understand.

I belong to the cloaked group of nerds devoted to our own particular branch of relentless research. We were in no way similar to one another. We found that fact comforting.

No one knew where we disappeared to at lunch or outside school hours. Some hid in the libraries. Some were in the science lab designing and building a computer. Some, like me, were in the art room creating murals to hang on the office counter. We loved our anonymity.

No one could see us unless there was a test coming up. I found it alarming when the cheerleader, football idol or the popular politician in my class headed straight toward me as we waited outside a locked classroom.

Inside the teacher would be putting test papers face down on each desk and erasing with vigor any trace of lessons still lingering on the board.

"What is going to be on the test?" they would whisper to me one after the other.

It was terrifying that they could even see me. It was startling when they got so close to my face and bent down to whisper in my ear. I was not used to such intimacy.

"Can I have a quick look at your notes? The Vice President of the Girl's Council would demand.

I dressed in clothing I made myself from a single pattern. It was a sheath dress that zipped up the back and had long sleeves down to my wrists. The collar was a round opening high up on my neck. Pictures from that time depict what looks like a 40-year-old ex-nun who has left the convent and is trying to wear civilian clothes. I was purposely austere.

Toward spring the others were buzzing with the important question: "Are you going to the prom?"

I had attended dances in past years but at the age of 13 I was tired of standing backed against a wall and willing my face to look weirdly ecstatic.

It was so like physical education. The public pillory of being one of the last two or three waiting to be chosen for a team.

Who would choose me?

And so I stopped going to the "hops" and the "socials". I had books at home and notes to take. I was reading *The Rime of the Ancient Mariner* out loud to myself in my bedroom.

Then one day, Stan walked straight up to me at my locker. He wasn't in any of my classes so I could in no way be of service to his academic success. I held on to my locker door for support. I was shocked. He had blonde hair and clear blue eyes behind silver rimmed glasses.

He was quite a bit taller than me even with his bent over posture.

"Is anybody taking you to the prom?" he asked me.

I stood very, very still and tried to understand the language he was speaking. I knew some of the words but not in that order. Time passed as I ran my mind over the sentence again and again.

"No," is what I said.

But I was thinking of the many times nobody had asked me for anything other than my notes. So many people had not asked me to dance, or join their team, or go to a movie. The list was forming in my mind of all the times I was uninvited.

He paused. I could tell he was struggling, and I felt sorry for both of us. Poor us.

"Will you go with me?"

He was dipping down below his status. He was asking a junior and a dour weirdo to go on a date with him.

When I got home, I was so excited I yelled at my mother.

"I am going to the spring prom. A BOY asked me."

She knew about these things because she had been "Susie Q ", the adorable girl in her school. They all loved her. She had so many dates, she told me over and over.

"I had ringlets all around my face. Several men proposed to me."

So, we went to the fancy-dress shop, and I tried on a white tulle skirted dress with a deep red velvet bodice. The traps were rhinestones and the bodice had rhinestones sprinkles randomly all over it. I was in love with the dress. I flounced and swished and sparkled and felt shockingly nude with my shoulders exposed.

When he arrived at the door, he was dressed in an expensive two-piece suit and held a plastic container out to me. He was quiet, diffident, and gentle. I didn't understand what he had brought for me, but my mother explained it was a wrist corsage. A single speckled orchid with a sweet smell was strapped to my left arm. I let him do it.

He could drive. He was a senior. And so, we got into his car. It was strange, all of it.

We didn't talk at all but just sat far away from each other.

The gym was decorated fiercely to look like something it could never be but by now I was in such a state of shock I did not even see the gym. I just felt the semi-nudity of my dress, the strange, elevated shoes on my feet and the smell of orchid, hair spray, after shave mingling.

We danced a few times, but I was focused on keeping him at a distance. I went stiff and defensive as he wrapped his arm around me. Running away from his body was my goal. How do I stay close to him, dance with him but not allow him to push his body into mine?

He tried to hold my hand as we stood at the edge of the festivities. I was with the normals. I was included and I hated it. I tried to talk to him but both of us were unskilled and awkward.

At the end of the dance, my bodice was sweat stained under the arms. I could see I was horrid. I was doing it all wrong as I watched other girls lay on their dates as if the partner was a chaise lounge. Other girls did tilting head, side glancing, hip swinging, radiant smiling. I was just so wrong for this.

When we got to my house, he parked outside and slid over on the seat. He put his arm behind me and bent down to kiss me. I averted my face. He moved closer and pulled me toward him. His lips got close to my face, and I turned away, so he landed on my left cheek.

He made little noises before saying," Oh come on. Don't you like me?"

"Yes. You are very nice," I said offering up the least possibly offensive thing I could say.

"Thank you, "I said as I opened my car door and extricated the white tulle from under him. "Thank you. That was fun. Thank you for asking me."

I repeated it because I was so relieved it was over. I didn't want to hold hands with someone I did not know or have his arm around my waist or his lower body pushed against me, or his lips on mine. I wanted to go into the house and read to calm myself down.

That was on a Saturday night, the big prom. On Monday morning my name came over the office loudspeaker. It was the principal's voice. "Cherie Coach, come to the office now."

I had never heard my name over the office broadcast system. I was invisible or good, existing along that spectrum all the years of middle school and high school. Only the offensive were called publicly to the office during class.

Every person in my class stared at me in surprise as I gathered my books to my chest like a breast plate. I walked past open doors and dozens of people sitting within observed my long journey.

I thought I would have to wait. But, no. The principal came out to the counter immediately and asked me to come in his office. He was a round, jovial man given to temper fits. Each student's description of him was different. It depended on something out of anyone's control, we decided.

As he spoke to me, leaning toward me, I suddenly understood.

Stan, he explained, had gone home from our date and hung himself in the attic. His parents were away for a few days. They found him there. Alone. He was still wearing the suit.

I began to understand that the interrogation was about what I had done to make a quiet boy kill himself. It was that way all day. First the principal, then the school counselor and finally during gym class as we did round dances… boy after boy would allemande toward me to ask.

"What did you do?"

Simone Blais's notes

This deftly crafted piece dissects high school cliques, and the challenge of achieving social mobility in a rigid hierarchy. The rich description of teenaged life in the lead up to prom, not to mention the dramatic conclusion, turned this coming-of-age story on its head with breath-taking results.

Prejudice & Necrotizing Enterocolitis

... Johanna Van Zanten

First Place

When I visited Canada for the first time in 1980, part of my month-long visit to a friend was attending the Assembly of the Northwest Territories' First Nations in Fort Good Hope—Dene Tha country. Darlene, the Indigenous girlfriend of an oil patch worker, had invited my friend and me along for the Pow-Wow at her grandmother's village. We packed up a freight canoe and took her, her white man, and their baby to her village downstream from Norman Wells on the mighty Mackenzie River.

We camped out by the river in our brand-new, white canvas tent, purchased at the only store. The CBC Radio crew and our group of three were the only non-Indigenous. This town of log homes, a few boxy social housing units, a church, and a school *was* the Hudson Bay Co. Darlene's grandmother arrived to get Darlene and kindly invited us to attend the communal meals. Young local activists took time to educate us, silly foreigners. I heard about the government's shocking abductions of children from their families and the complete betrayal of treaty rights. I met some local leaders and would never forget the man named after the great Dutch humanist, Erasmus. The assembly of representatives elected George Erasmus as their new leader.

Over the four days of my stay, I became spellbound by the people, their meetings and praying rituals in the willow pole enclosure, the lovely communal meals, wild meat roasted over the in-ground pits, and the hand games, the drumming, chanting and dancing at the school gym each night till midnight. I listened to the wolves howl in answer to the sled dogs, tied up by their dens in front of every home.

The events took place in a sober state, as the area was dry, surveillance by the locals. My attachment to Canada's First Nations was born then and there. I became their advocate in a white world full of Canadian prejudice.

Two years later, I landed as a new immigrant in a small town in Central Alberta. I watched CBC's First Ministers' Conference broadcast in 1983, transfixed, full of hope. George Erasmus pleaded eloquently for First Nations' right to self-government and a place at the table. Yet, Pierre Trudeau didn't think that making space for the Indigenous in this political forum would benefit the country. With the First Ministers Conferences deleted from the agenda a few years later, the question became moot. The provinces became ever less attached to the idea of unity, preferring to chart their own course.

In 1986, I landed a maternity backfill job as a play therapist for vulnerable children in northern Alberta, an area of remote Indigenous communities and reserves surrounding Slave Lake. The play sessions happened at their homes, so I met up weekly with Indigenous and white families.

One of my clients was preemie Lily with her sweetest family of all. Will was in his early forties, a hunter-trapper and a quiet man, tall and gentle. His wife, Candace, nineteen, was the beautiful and loving mother of their three-year old, robust son Johnny and their newborn daughter. Lily survived her pending birth at 28 weeks of gestation with a helicopter ride to the Edmonton hospital and the interventions from technological gadgets in the NICU. She came home at three months old—really her ninth month of gestation. I met her when she was one year old.

This quiet Indigenous family became dear to me during our working together in weekly sessions at their home. Candace was Will's second wife. Their home was an old log home on the flats by the river with a wood stove for heating. With her sensitive, premature lungs, wood heating was not good for Lily, so the Health Unit financed the replacement gas heater. They lived a simple and sober life off the land. Fishing, hunting, and trapping, and seasonal berry gathering provided what they needed, with the occasional supplement from the welfare office.

Lily was growing steadily, somewhat hampered by physical immaturity. She didn't like to stretch tall and showed a marked preference for one side of her body. She had a scar on her tummy from the feeding tube inserted at birth, as she had not matured enough for oral feeds.

That spring, Will gladly took the two black rabbits off my hands—gifts from a neighbour for my preschool daughter. Due to my ignorance, I had lost their first unanticipated litter, born in the depth of winter. I found the naked bodies frozen solid in the bare run and realized only then the bunnies had been buck and doe. From then on, I had kept the lovelorn cottontails inside our shed in separate cages—leftover junk from an abandoned mink farm.

A year after my job finished, Will and Candace visited me unexpectedly with Johnny. After the initial greetings, I immediately asked where Lily was.

"We want to tell you about Lily," Candace said quietly. Will's face dropped, and he glanced away into the distance. He looked older and more tired than I remembered. Candace had also lost some of her shine.

"Come, Johnny, we'll check out the back forty," Will said. Candace nodded.

"Fiddleheads grow there," I said. The tall man and his son walked off through the backyard and into the adjacent stand of birches.

"Let's go in, we'll have some tea," I offered. Candace agreed.

Inside, I put the kettle on, and we sat down at the kitchen table. Candace rummaged in her purse: she had something for me and stretched out her hand. I took it. At first glance, I couldn't identify the print on stiff paper, the size of a recipe card, but then it struck me. I was a diminutive print of a baby's left foot—Lily's.

"Oh, no, what happened?" I groaned. "Is this Lily's?"

Candace nodded. "From when she was born. In case she would die I would have something to remember her by. You can have it. I have another print."

With few words, she told me in a calm but monotone voice that Lily had been ill, and she brought her to the hospital. The child had not wanted to eat that morning, started vomiting, and was unusually quiet the whole day, just laying around on the floor, and she developed a fever around dinnertime. It was a Friday evening. As she was waiting for her turn, Candace heard a nurse talk to another in the treatment room. She said something like, *Oh boy, another mom who wants to go drinking, looking for a babysitter.* Then she was called in. The emergency nurse had a look and asked some questions but didn't ask a doctor to see Lily and sent them home with the conclusion that Lily had the flu and would perk up the next day.

By midnight, Lily was very ill, didn't move at all, and seemed unconscious. This time, Will came along to the emergency ward and insisted the nurse getting a doctor. As soon as the doctor-on-call arrived and saw Lily undressed, he asked questions about her birth. Lily was flown to the Edmonton hospital in the emergency helicopter. Candance was allowed to accompany her, but Will had to drive to Edmonton himself. "When he arrived, Lily had already died from poisoning," signed Candace. "Her whole body had been infected from a blocked intestine."

I was devastated, shocked by this terrible callousness, the injustice of it all.

"Candace, how horrible. What a terrible nurse. How could they not believe you when you first came to emergency? You are Lily's mother, you *knew* what's going on. They could have saved Lily."

She shrugged. "It happens a lot. They think we're stupid. We don't drink. Others might, but we're a sober Native family. Will lost his first family because of alcohol. He learned to be sober."

Teary-eyed, I hugged her. "I am so sorry this happened to you. It shouldn't have. That nurse was stupid. What did Angela say?" She was the therapist I backfilled for.

"I didn't tell her what the nurse said. Angela said it is a common thing with premature babies." Candace looked so helpless; she broke my heart.

I realized Candace had not wanted to inconvenience her regular worker, but I couldn't accept that.

"I am sure it is not common the babies die from it. The hospital knew about Lily's prematurity, her scar, and the direct feeding tube. It's all in her file. They should've known. I bet the nurse didn't check the records. You can sue them for their negligence. Lily's death might have been prevented. Do you want me to do something, call Angela, or call a lawyer?" I put my hand on her knee.

This was the old story of racism, the denial that the Indigenous can be capable parents, the prejudice that all Native parents are drunks. Well, the Slave Lake hospital proved that they still were thinking along colonial lines. My anger rising, I was ready to prove them wrong.

Candace looked at me with sad eyes. She shook her head. "Nothing will come of it. It won't bring Lily back. We just have to accept it and live on with her gone. I'm not angry. Will is, but I'm not. It's just life."

"Candace, you are a terrific mom. Look at Johnny, such a stout and strong boy. A premature birth wasn't your fault and you looked after Lily so well. I wished I had been there for you. Thank you for letting me know about what happened. I'm so sorry." I was crying by then, of anger, of grief.

We drank our tea in silence as I desperately tried to get hold of myself. I blamed Angela, the play therapist—another white Canadian who failed her client. When will this disaster of prejudice so soaked into the mainstream social fabric finally disappear? Even my own husband, with a crush on Suzi—Indigenous water-hauler at his work—happily made "jokes" with his friends using his imitation Native accent, denying his liberal upbringing. Does one have to be a racist to fit in? Granted, I only was an ignorant new immigrant at that time, but this part I resented wholeheartedly, and still do. It's unforgivable.

"Will you be alright, Candace? Is there anything I can do?"

She shook her head and pushed her hair out of her face. "I will be okay. Johnny misses her. Will is taking him out lots. He likes the beach and all the sand. Me too, and then I go with them."

"That's good." I was looking for a thing to say that may be useful but didn't find anything.

We heard the voices of Will and Johnny nearing the open front door. Candace got up. "Thanks for the tea, Johanna," she said.

"Do you want some vegetables? Come to the garden and see. We have too much anyway." I put the card with Lily's footprint on the shelf, out of reach of my toddler, still napping. We met Will and Johnny by the door, and together, we ambled to the garden on the other side of the house.

That spring, I had removed much sod from our vast lawn to enlarge the veggie garden to four times its original size. Everything grew fast with the extended daylight when the sun didn't go down till eleven. I was proud of my asparagus. After growing crops in central Alberta for a few years, the north astonished me with what survived in winters of 35-below. The bears liked my garden, too, but that's alright. They were here first.

Indigenous Canadians have that same resilience. Despite settlers and the government trying to wipe them out, they survived for centuries. I loaded Candace and Will up with veggies, feeling vastly inadequate and humbled by their grace.

The name of the preemie condition is Necrotizing Enterocolitis, but prejudice killed Lily. I will never forget her.

Simone Blais's notes

This a devastating story contributing to the current discourse on social justice. Canada is seen through the eyes of a newcomer, and that unflinching stare lays bare systemic racism against Indigenous people. The narrator's righteous anger, contrasted with the mother's resigned grief, forces the reader to confront the gut-wrenching reality that the experience of Joyce Echaquan in Canadian hospitals is not isolated.

Copyrights

Fiction

The Day Jesus Came to Work

© 2021 Svea Benson

Sweek Michael Sky

© 2021 Andrea Heidebrecht

Fat Friday

© 2021 Garry Litke

The Rhee Family Drugstore

© 2021 Finnian Burnett

Poetry

Non-Fiction

Eocene Walk

© 2021 Donald V. Gayton

Stan, Alone in the Attic

© 2021 Cherie Hanson

Prejudice & Necrotizing Enterocolitis

© 2021 Johanna Van Zanten

More

For more, go to ThePrairieSoul.com/press

PRAIRIE SOUL PRESS

Manufactured by Amazon.ca
Bolton, ON

27376220R00044